. _____ Br?

?rl?   ?ont

WITHDRAWN
FROM
STOCK

THIS WALKER BOOK BELONGS TO:

_____

_____

_____

_____

D1340736

For Amelia – P. R.
For my brother, Rob – C. D.

First published 2002 by Walker Books Ltd
87 Vauxhall Walk, London SE11 5HJ

This edition published 2003

10 9 8 7 6 5 4 3 2 1

Text © 2002 Phyllis Root
Illustrations © 2002 Christopher Denise

This book has been typeset in Kennerley

Printed in China

All rights reserved. No part of this book may be reproduced,
transmitted or stored in an information retrieval system
in any form or by any means, graphic, electronic or mechanical,
including photocopying, taping and recording,
without prior written permission from the publisher.

British Library Cataloguing in Publication Data:
a catalogue record for this book
is available from the British Library

ISBN 0-7445-9841-9

www.walkerbooks.co.uk

OLiVeR
FiNDS HiS WAY

Phyllis Root

illustrated by

Christopher Denise

WALKER BOOKS
AND SUBSIDIARIES
LONDON · BOSTON · SYDNEY · AUCKLAND

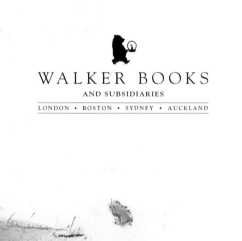

3014405

Leabharlann
Contae na Mhise

While Mother Bear hangs out the washing
and Father Bear rakes the leaves,
Oliver chases a big yellow leaf ...

down the hill,

round a clumpy bush,

under a twisty tree,
and all the way
to the edge of the wood.

Oliver looks for the
yellow leaf.
He can't see it.
Oliver looks for his house.
No house.
Mother Bear? Father Bear?
Oliver thinks,
and he begins to run.

Oliver runs to a tree.

That's not the twisty tree!

He runs to a bush.

That's not the clumpy bush!

All alone at the edge of
the wood,
Oliver starts to cry.
Oliver is lost.

Oliver cries
and cries.

Oliver is still lost.

Oliver rubs his nose
and thinks.

He thinks
and thinks.

Then, all alone at the
edge of the wood,
Oliver has an idea.

"*Roar!*"

"*Roar!*"

"Roar!"

From far away,
under a twisty tree,
round a clumpy bush,
and all the way up the hill,
Oliver hears Mother Bear
roar back.
Oliver hears Father Bear
roar back.

Oliver runs and runs,
under the twisty tree,

round the clumpy bush,

up the hill,
all the way
to his very own house
with a pile of leaves
and washing on
the line.

All the way to

Mother Bear and Father Bear

who have warm bear hugs ...

just for Oliver.

Leabharlann
Jo 14405
Comac na Midhe